Mirror

By: Deshune Heard- Watkins
Illustrated by: Tiffany Davis

THIS BOOK IS INSPIRED BY MY DAUGHTER AND IS DEDICATED TO MY YOUNGER SELF. IN LIFE WE ARE INSPIRED BY MANY THINGS THAT AFFECT US MENTALLY, EMOTIONALLY AND SPIRITUALLY. IT IS HOWEVER ALWAYS IN THE FINAL MOMENTS WHEN HOPES SEEM TO BE LOST THAT WE HAVE TO DIG DEEP AND BE OUR BIGGEST INSPIRATION AND MOTIVATION. TO ENCOURAGE YOURSELF IS THE GREATEST DEFINITION OF STRENGTH. IT BUILDS CHARACTER AND ENHANCES YOUR INNER STRENGTH. IT IS THAT STRENGTH THAT GIVES YOU POWER AND MAKES YOU A SURVIVOR.

GROWING UP, I WAS BLESSED WITH MANY TOOLS OF LIFE, SOME EASY, SOME HARD; I HAD PEOPLE TO POUR GOOD AND BAD THINGS IN ME— SOME OF THE THINGS WANTED TO BUILD ME WHILE SOME AIMED TO TEAR ME DOWN —BUT I HAD THE FINAL SAY. I HAD TO LEARN A NEW DEFINITION OF HOW I WOULD LOVE MYSELF. I HAD TO TRUST MYSELF AND BELIEVE IN MYSELF NO MATTER WHAT —NO ONE WANTED ME TO WIN MORE THAN ME. THE MIRROR WAS THE BEST WAY TO CONNECT WITH MY INNER SELF....IT WAS MY SAFE ZONE, MY POWER ZONE, MY WAY TO REBOOT, TO POWER UP AND KEEP GOING.

"THE BEST WAY TO IDENTIFY YOU IS TO SEE YOURSELF."
- SHUN WATKINS

MONDAY

Oh mirror! Oh mirror! It's me, well, of course, who else would it be.

And YAZZZZ! I feel absolutely fabulous. Thanks for asking! I mean why wouldn't I...?

I am as light as a feather; can fly high as a bird; strong as a lion and tough as a Harpy eagle claw.

I am great! I am bold! I am strong, and I am kind. I am everything of amazing.

Momma always said I can be anything I want to be, I can make the impossible possible, and I can make mountains move if I push hard enough.

Now does she actually mean I can really move a mountain... Nahhhh! I doubt it, but hey, you get the picture, Right...?

Would you look at the day?

It's as nice as my favorite caramel-vanilla-cookie-crunch ice-cream. It's as pretty as my mother on Sunday mornings. I mean it's so pretty; pretty enough to have a backyard showdown, in other words a bar-be-que. If only there were enough hours in a day. I wish I had time to take a spin on the swing, hang out with my girls at the park, shoot some hoops and have a little girl talk but, a girl got business to attend to, and that's that. I have gymnastics at 10, study hall at 1 and basketball practice at 4....

Oh Monday, Oh Monday, from the look of things, you are going to be a busy but great day for me! I've got this. I've got this in a bag.

WELL HELLO
TUESDAY

I can tell you one thing, today is definitely not yesterday. Hmmm, this ought to be quite interesting.

Today is wet, rainy, and gloomy and it's a bit of a flood out there. Chances of me feeling wet, icky and slimy are way above 90 percent. **UGHHHH YUCK!**

But, in the words of my mother, "Bills are still due, schools are still open, and my job requires me to clock in. So get a move on it Moo-moo."

Yeah, it's silly I know..., She calls me Moo-moo. But never mind that. Let's just act like you didn't hear that.

FOCUS! Why don't you, FOCUS! We have way more important things to worry about.

LIKE...

The RAIN people, The RAIN....

I know it's wet; I know it's rainy; I know it's gloomy, but it is nothing a good ole raincoat and rain boots can't handle.

Okay, take a deep breath, let's just calm down. I can handle it. I mean, I'm quite smart, if I do say so myself. I've got this. This is going to be easy. I am going to breeze through Tuesday with a BANG.

Even if my raincoat looks a tad bit strange, has a weird little smell, makes this ridiculously annoying noise when I walk, and let's not forget, it is as bright as the sun, and makes it impossible to miss me, I still love it, and, I guess it gets the job done. Oh, but let's not forget my favorite umbrella and my adorable rain boots.

I've got this. I've got this in a bag.

HEY! WHAT'S UP WEDNESDAY

How you Doing? It sholl is shining mighty bright out there today.

It's Hump day! Its hump day! It's the middle of the week! It's hump day!

Ayeeeee....
Shine bright like a diamond.

Okay, Wednesday, I see you. You clean up quite nicccccely.

I can tell this is going to be a sunglasses, tan lotion, shorts and flip flops kind of day. No sun that my good ole sunglasses can't block. I got this!

This is going to be so easy baby!

Maybe I can be nice and make Ice cream with Trever, my little brother. He can sure enough drive me crazy, but truthfully he actually is pretty cool. I guess.

But don't you dare tell him I said that.

So I decided to hit the town with my baby brother, and dude....We are wayyy exhausted. I mean, we played basketball, flew kites, chased flies, played hopscotch and ate homemade ice cream, made by me, your girl Jazz, of course. Man ohh- man! Nothing like homemade vanilla ice cream on a cone. Hmmmmm, Deeeelicious! Today was so AWE-some! Boy, did we have a blast!

GOOD OLE THURSDAY

I think today would be a good day to sleep in. Geeeesss! I am still tired from yesterday. Oh Mirror, oh mirror! LOOK AT ME, I look a mess. A cute mess, though. And poor Trever, he still has his play clothes on from yesterday. He must have been really tired. Ewww, now that's nasty. But he is my baby brother, so he gets a pass.

Oh but wait....

Hey! We have some chores to do; a whole list of them. Boy oh boy! What are we going to do? I'm freaking out here.

Chores oh chores go away! Please come back another day.

Trever whispers as he yarns, "Oh Jazz, don't worry about it. If we work together, we can make it happen. And stop pacing the floor already. PLEASE, you are making me nervous. You are going to drive me nuts, Gees!"

You're right; there is nothing to it but to do it. I'm going to turn on some happy music and get a move on it.

HAPPPY PEOPLE IN THE
AIRRRR....... AYYYYEEEE!
We've got this; we've got this in a bag.

WELL GOODBYE THURSDAY AND HELLO FRIDAY!

I guess it's true what they say, there is nothing like waking up to a clean ole house. Smelling like good ole pine sol. Hmm, wait a minute. Oh Mirror, oh Mirror! It sure smells good downstairs. I smell bacon, sausage, eggs... not any ole kind of eggs, but sweet ole cheese eggs. Mmmmm! Can someone say BREAKFAST, YAZZZ. If my nose sensors me correctly, I think I smell pancakes too. I mean, is today a special holiday or something? Surely, could've fooled me.

TUH! Silly me, I'm just joking around. Nana cooks breakfast every day, and lunch, and dinner. I mean, she cooks like it's a holiday or something. She even makes us special snacks, like cakes and pies. Some things Nana just make up as she goes; I can't tell you half of what it's called, but they are yummy to my tummy, and that's all that matters. My momma says, she's spoiled us rotten. This may very well be true. But, isn't that what Nanas are for?

Fridays are FUNdays! My mommy calls it, "Go for what you want Fridays." We get to relax, eat what we want and stay up all night long. No chores, no cleaning, no nothing. Just relaxing.

Oh Friday, oh Friday! I feel like Kevin Durant and Skylar Diggins Baby! I think I'll go shoot some hoops today. No relaxing here. I'll save that for later. Are you coming to join me, Trever? "Yep, I'm already ready; feeling like Lebron James BABY!"

Whewww! That was fun. I'm exhausted. What about you Trever? "Yep, but, I can't wait to see what Nana has whipped up for us. I hope she made some of those brownies with strawberries and whip cream on top. Those are my favorites." Nooo! What about those pecan swirly things, with the white icing on the top. "Oh yeaaaa! I forgot about those. They are my second favorites." **LAST ONE TO THE HOUSE IS A ROTTEN EGG!** "Wait, wait up Jazz." "Let's go Trever, catch up, you can do it!"

BOOOOOOM!

TREVER, are you okay? "I think so. I fell pretty hard Jazz and it burns really bad." I'm so sorry but don't you worry. Wait here, I'll be back in a jiffy.

ZOOOOOOM...Zooooooooom....

See, I'm back, that didn't take so long now, did it? "Noooooo, I guess not." I know it hurts, and I know it burns. It will only last for a few more seconds. A little peroxide, ointment and a bandage should do the trick. It will be over before you know it.

Now you fan and I'll pour … and finish it off with a bandage.

BAMMMM, all done. See.… You are as good as new. "Wow, thanks Jazz! I feel so much better. And you know what would make me feel even better?" Yep! I think I do. Some good ole brownies, with strawberries and whip cream to top it off. "Yep, it would make my fall sooooooo worth it." Hahaha! All set Lebron James? "Yep, all set." Well, in that case, let us get a move on it.

Oh, I almost forgot. Look what I have, Trever....

SUPRISEEEEEE... I've got PIEEEEEEE... MMMM... YOUR FAVORITE!

See Trever, we got this; we've got this in a bag. "Now that's quite allll-right, so quite alright. Thanks Jazz. Today is officially a good day!" You're welcome, Trever, now let's get home kiddo.

COME ON IN SATURDAY

Whooowwww! What a day, what a night! Man ole man I am sooooo tired. Yesterday was everything amazing minus that little booboo with Trever, but he is as good as new. Today I would rather chill in my favorite PJ's, eat my favorite popcorn, and watch my favorite movies. But hey that's just me, wishful thinking!

Mom says today we are going fishing with Uncle Luke. Uncle Luke, fishing! What is the fun in that? Oh Mirror oh mirror! I've never gone fishing before: slimy fish, long polls, and yucky worms. Who does that? Oh my, oh my!
It's going to be one heck of a day. What a Bomber.

I guess I better slide on these yellow boots and this weird looking hat Nana bought - THE HUNTING HAT....At least I will look "a fisher," I think. Oh well, Uncle Luke will be here before we know it. Better tell Trever to put a move on it. Mirror, wish me luck!

Man, Uncle Luke....It is mighty quiet out here; feels like we are in the middle of nowhere. Oh my, these are going to be the longest hours of my life.

"O! Little one, hush. You will be alright, trust me, it will be worth your while."

I don't know Uncle Luke. These bugs are annoying, and this water has a very weird smell, and I mean it in the worst way.

"Huhuhu! Girl, you are such a handful and a tad bit funny, I must add."

Ughh, welp! I guess, we going fishing. Let's get going Unc. We got this; we've got this in a bag!

Oh mirror oh mirror, I can't believe I actually went fishing. I mean, I CAUGHT A FISH! I couldn't believe it....And though it was super quiet, I mean really, really quiet, it was actually pretty dope. We listened to some throwback stories of Uncle Luke and Momma when they were youngins'. We watched Uncle Luke clean, scale and cook the fish right before our eyes. And the fish was deeeeelicious.

Even though the slimy, slippery little fella grossed me out a little, it was cool at the same time. The experience was bomb dot com!

Now, it's time to get out of these stinky sticky clothes, smelling like old chitterlings in sewage water, Wheeww, now, that's just funky!

Shower to the rescue.... SHOWER!

Goodnight Beautiful, You Rock!

Gooooodnight....

GOOD OLE SUNDAY

I guess hanging out with Uncle Luke wasn't so bad, after all. Who am I kidding, it was amazing. Trever was so excited, he talked himself to sleep. I can't wait for our next fishing adventure with Uncl Luke. Next time, I'll remember to bring bug spray. Those bugs were not very pleasant They were very disrespectful. Welp.

Anywho...."GooooodmornTing Sunday!" I hear mom playing her inspirational music downstairs. You know the kind that speaks to your soul and all.

Sundays are pretty cool at "Th Pritchett's residence." Mom is usually off work on Sundays. Uncle Luke and his wife Ann would come over; Uncle Jae, mom's baby brother and Auntie Elaine, momma's best friend and a few cousins stop by

1449
Hattie
Road

Pritchett's Residence

from time to time; of course, Nana cooks a
big deeeliciious, over the top dinner each
Sunday. We get to spend time together,
eat good food and play family games....

We've been doing this as long as I can
remember. Maybe one day I will do this
with my family.

But just like any other family, what's a
day with family without a little drama
Geeezlaweeze! Cousin Earl and Uncle Jae
are arguing over what movie is better
And poor Ms. Ann, she's always saying
"Well, well boys! Just pick one already."
It's so funny, because after about 20
minutes of going back and forth, Momma
yells out, "Give the remote to Jazz, she wil
pick one until you boys get it together."
Auntie Elaine mostly sits there and
laughs, saying, "That is just a shame; they
do this all the time."

I think they miss each other way mor
than they would like to admit. But it's
okay, you can always count on Jazz to
pick a good movie and shut everyone up.

I either pick a good ole action movie or one of my mother's classics from the 90's, - everyone loves "Jerry Maguire," "Boyz N The Hood" and the all-time family favorite, "Soul Food." As my great Granny use to say, with "Good food and a good movie, Chileee, is as quiet as a mouse." I mean you could hear a pin drop, right up until cousin Earl and Uncle Jae decide to argue over the last piece of cornbread, or in-between Trever loud smacking; for the most part it is pretty quiet. Family is everything to my Momma. She always says, "Family is what you make it." Tuh, family can drive you crazy, but I love them anyway.

At least I have to.

"It's Picture Tiiiiime"….

Ole boy, here goes cousin Earl with his old 1967 camera. 1, 2, 3…. He runs to make the picture before it gets to 5. He just refuses to upgrade and get in touch with the tech world. I don't understand why he loves that old camera so much. But hey, that's cousin Earl for you!

Even though we have phones and all this good technology, he still makes us take a picture with that old camera. "Memories! Life is all about memories," is his favorite quote, right before he takes 3 big ole to-go plates out the door. Mmm, mmm, mmm, cousin Earl is so funny.

"Bye-bye everyone, thank you for coming, see you next Sunday, and bring some drinks next time, and Earl, bring your own to-go plates and foil," Momma yells out the door. Chuckling as she closes the door behind them.

"Good ole family time! It's a sure enough mess sometimes, but it's always a good time."

Goodnight Momma. Goodnight Nana, love you; thank you for all you do. I'm going to bed.

Family makes me exhausted. "Me too," "Me three," but family is a beautiful thing.

"Goodnight Jazz, I love you beautiful."

Oh mirror, oh mirror! Family day was quite alright. It's not always a perfect Sunday.... TUH, who am I kidding? It's never a perfect Sunday, but I love every bit of it. Look at that picture, we look good. We look real good. It looks just perfect to me. My great Granny always says, "Be patient, be kind and be relaxed; spend time with family and do EVERYTHING with LOVE."

And on that note, it's time to shower up, put on my favorite PJ's and tuck it on in.

Oh Mirror, oh mirror! This was a pretty awesome week. We breezed through like a CHAMP! GIRRRRLLL! We got it going on. We Rock! We are awesome, and can do anything we put our mind to because we are just that great! We are brave, strong, and smart and everything we need to be. Tuh! I am beautiful from the inside out, from the top of my head, on down to my pretty little feet. We got this. We got this in the bag. Peace and

GOOOOOOOOOOOOOOOOOOOODNIGHT with your gorgeous self. Monday, get ready, because here I come!

NOW MONDAY

WHERE YOU AT...

About the Illustrator

My name is Tiffany Davis. I am originally from Kingston, Jamaica, and I've lived in Atlanta, Georgia most of my life. I've always been an Artist at heart, and I started drawing at a very young age. I was an Apprentice Artist for ArtsCool, a summer job in high school where I enhanced my drawing skills. I always wanted to learn painting but never had the opportunity until my later years and now, I continue to teach myself. I practice my painting skills almost daily, and I have been taking custom orders for years now, which has helped me to achieve so many of my goals. I'm also a painting instructor and an illustrator.

Deshune` Heard- Watkins

Shun Watkins was born and raised in Atlanta, GA. She is a mother of three- two boys and one girl. She received an Associate's Degree from Atlanta Technical College in Early Childhood Education; she received her Bachelor's Degree from Mercer University in Communication. She is a jack of many trades. Some of her favorite hobbies are writing poetry, horseback riding and cooking. Writing has always been dear and near to her heart, used to express her feelings and emotions; but it also became a tool that saved her life.

Although writing is something I do daily, to free my mind or to simply jot down my emotions, I never thought in a million years I would write a book for children. For three days, my mind was moving 200 miles per hour, and I would wake up at 4am. I kept asking God why are you waking me up this early, I barely get any sleep. I'm working two jobs, going to school, and being a full time parent. Lord my plate is full. By the 4th day at 4 am, I opened my laptop and started writing, with no vision, no road map.3 hours later I was halfway on my journey to completing my very first book. With no clue and no direction, I sat in the library for hours and days reading different children's book. For months, I would ask myself, "What if the book doesn't do great, what if it's not good enough or what if it sounds silly?" A loud voice said, if it was placed in your heart, it is yours to fulfill.

"Oh Mirror, Oh Mirror! Fear is not my future. Fear does not own me nor can it consume me—for I am everything I need to be and everything I shall be"~Shun Watkins

CPSIA information can be obtained
at www.ICGtesting.com
Printed in the USA
LVHW070134281020
669821LV00007BA/69

9 781735 386621